Jonathan Bean
Building Our House

Farrar Straus Giroux
New York

Farrar Straus Giroux Books for Young Readers
175 Fifth Avenue, New York 10010

Copyright © 2013 by Jonathan Bean
Color separations by Embassy Graphics Ltd.
Printed in China by RR Donnelley Asia Printing Solutions Ltd.,
Dongguan City, Guangdong Province
Designed by Jay Colvin
First edition, 2013
7 9 10 8 6

mackids.com

Library of Congress Cataloging-in-Publication Data
Bean, Jonathan, 1979–
    Building our house / Jonathan Bean. — 1st ed.
        p.   cm.
    Summary: A young girl narrates her family's move from the city
to the country, where they have bought a piece of land and live in a trailer
while they build a house from the ground up, with help from relatives
and friends.
    ISBN 978-0-374-38023-6 (hardcover)
    [1. House construction—Fiction.   2. Building—Fiction.   3. Family
life—Fiction.]   I. Title.

PZ7.B3664Bui 2013
[E]—dc23

                                                        2012004993

Today is moving day. We left our old house in the city and are moving to the country.

My family is building our new house away from the road,
back down a dirt lane.

Our house will sit in the middle of a weedy field Dad and Mom
bought from a farmer.

My family makes up a strong crew of four and we have a truck named Willys. My brother helps Dad carry the tools. "The right tools for the right job," says Dad.

I help Mom carry the plans. "A good plan for a good house,"
says Mom. Willys carries everything else.

A truck towing a trailer pulls into the field. The trailer has a door, two windows, and a chimney. Dad tells the driver to park the trailer under an oak tree.

The next day, a truck with a tall rig pulls into the field. It has a long drill that can bore through dirt and rock, down to fresh water. The men who drive the truck lay pipes that will carry the water to the trailer.

The day after that, a truck with a bucket pulls into the field. It has a long arm that moves the bucket up and down. A man in the bucket works cautiously with wires that will carry electricity to the trailer.

We will live in this small home on wheels while we build our new house.

During the week Dad goes to his job in town, but on the weekend he starts up Willys and everyone jumps in. We go to buy stacks of lumber from the sawmill.

We collect piles of rock from our neighbor's pasture.

We bring loads of sand and stone from the quarry.

We gather supplies with Willys until the weedy field is filled
with stacks and piles and loads of what we need to start building.

On a clear, cold night Dad sets the corners of the foundation by the North Star.

One wall will face north to ward off the wind, one east to
welcome the morning, one south to soak in the sun, and one west
to see out the day.

When the weather warms, the ground softens and Grandpa visits with his backhoe. "Are you ready to dig?" he calls.

Grandpa follows the corners Dad placed, gently moving the levers that control the giant hoe.

He digs and dumps, scoops and piles, until there is a square hole in the field. This will be our new basement.

Dad saws boards that Mom hammers and nails into a form that will hold concrete and rock.

The concrete and rock will shape the foundation that will support the frame and make for a solid house.

Dad lays rocks one on top another while we fill the loud mixing machine. One shovel of cement, three shovels of sand, five of stone, and water till it's soupy.

The machine rumbles, tumbling the ingredients into concrete. Mom pours the concrete into a wheelbarrow and then dumps the wet mixture into the form.

When the concrete hardens, the form comes down and the foundation stands solid.

My brother helps Dad inspect the lumber. "Strong lumber for a strong frame," says Dad.

I help Mom mark the lumber that Dad will saw. "Measure twice to get it right," says Mom.

A drill, a chisel, and a mallet are the right tools to shape the lumber so that each piece fits snuggly into the next.

When every beam is marked and sawed and snug, we throw a big party.

A frame-raising party!

Everyone visits. My grandfather and grandmother, my aunts and uncles and cousins, my other grandfather and grandmother, my great-grandfather, our neighbors, and the workers from the sawmill and quarry make up a big frame-raising crew.

Our crew works until the sun sets and the frame stands strong in the middle of the field. Mom makes places for everyone to sit around a fire. We eat and talk and play until the stars shine and the owls call.

Now the weather cools. "Fall is here," says Mom. "Winter is coming," says Dad. We work harder than ever because the house needs a chimney and roof, siding and windows before the winter arrives.

But this year the first frost arrives early.

The cold rains fall early.

The icy winds that carry
the heavy snow blow early.

The bad weather slows our
work but doesn't stop it.

When the snow is deep Dad hooks a plow up to Willys.

He clears the driveway so that we can go to town and buy a stove.

The stove warms the house while we start our work inside. Our plans show us where to place walls that will make the rooms.

We plumb while the wind howls.

And wire while drifts pile up.

We insulate while the days grow shorter.

And then wallboard as they gradually grow longer.

We work on weekends.

We work in the evenings.

We work while Dad is at his job.

And then finally it's time for another party.

A moving party!

This time when everyone visits we have a big moving crew.
They bring rugs and chairs and lamps and help us empty out the
house-on-wheels so that a truck can pull it away.

Our big crew moves everything into the house.

When Mom and Dad are busy, I show the crew where things go.

Once the moving is done everyone goes back to their homes, but my family stays right where we are.

It's our very first night in our new home.

Author's Note

This book is dedicated to my family and is based on my parents' experience of buying an old field and living in a small house-on-wheels while they worked on building a house for their family. Instead of a year and a half, as in this story, it took every scrap of spare time and five years to complete. During those five years my parents had three children: two of my three sisters and me. Though I have vague memories of ladders and a cement mixer and a frame raising that have, no doubt, been enhanced by photographs my parents took (including the one of me above), this book's story is told from my older sister's point of view.

My parents thought of themselves as homesteaders and brought to house-building a pioneering spirit of ingenuity and independence. They decided to build a timber-frame house after reading a book on the subject, and it's true they collected rocks from a pasture, poured cellar walls with countless loads of cement from a small mixer, and bored holes in hard oak beams with an old-fashioned bit and brace. Of course, a homestead would not be complete without a large garden, fruit trees, pets, woodland, and a stream flowing through mysterious marshland. Add to that the wise love of two parents, the companionship of three sisters, and a practically lived faith, and it's hard for me to think of a better place to have grown up.